Frog and Toad
All Year

by Arnold Lobel

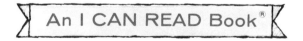

An I CAN READ Book®

HarperCollins*Publishers*

To James Marshall

HarperCollins®, 🐦®, and I Can Read Book® are
trademarks of HarperCollins Publishers Inc.

A portion of this book previously appeared in *Cricket*.

Frog and Toad All Year
Copyright © 1976 by Arnold Lobel
Printed in the U.S.A. All rights reserved.
www.harperchildrens.com

Library of Congress Cataloging-in-Publication Data
Lobel, Arnold.
  Frog and toad all year.
  (An I can read book)
  Summary: Two friends share experiences in each season of the year.
  [1. Friendship—Fiction. 2. Frogs—Fiction. 3. Toads—Fiction.] I. Title.
PZ7.L7795Fg3   [E]   76-2343
ISBN 0-06-023950-6
ISBN 0-06-023951-4 (lib. bdg.)
ISBN 0-06-444059-1 (pbk.)

Contents

Down the Hill

Frog knocked at Toad's door.

"Toad, wake up," he cried.

"Come out and see

how wonderful the winter is!"

"I will not," said Toad.

"I am in my warm bed."

"Winter is beautiful,"

said Frog.

"Come out and have fun."

"Blah," said Toad.

"I do not have

any winter clothes."

Frog came into the house.

"I have brought you
some things to wear," he said.

Frog pushed a coat
down over the top of Toad.

Frog pulled snowpants
up over the bottom of Toad.

He put a hat and scarf

on Toad's head.

"Help!" cried Toad.

"My best friend

is trying to kill me!"

"I am only getting you ready

for winter," said Frog.

Frog and Toad went outside.

They tramped through the snow.

"We will ride

down this big hill

on my sled," said Frog.

"Not me," said Toad.

"Do not be afraid," said Frog.

"I will be with you

on the sled.

It will be a fine, fast ride.

Toad, you sit in front.

I will sit right behind you."

The sled began to move

down the hill.

"Here we go!"

said Frog.

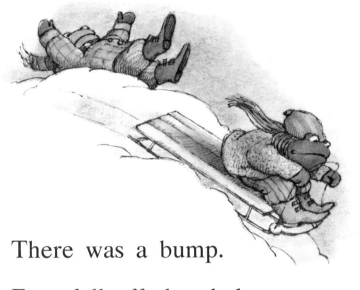

There was a bump.

Frog fell off the sled.

Toad rushed past trees and rocks.

"Frog, I am glad

that you are here," said Toad.

Toad leaped over

a snowbank.

"I could not steer the sled

without you, Frog," he said.

"You are right. Winter is fun!"

A crow flew nearby.

"Hello Crow," shouted Toad.

"Look at Frog and me.

We can ride a sled

better than anybody

in the world!"

12

"But Toad," said the crow,

"you are alone on the sled."

Toad looked around.

He saw that Frog was not there

"I AM ALL ALONE!"

screamed Toad.

Bang!

The sled hit a tree.

Thud!

The sled hit a rock.

14

Plop!

The sled dived

into the snow.

15

Frog came running down the hill.

He pulled Toad out of the snow.

"I saw everything," said Frog.

"You did very well

by yourself."

"I did not," said Toad.

"But there is one thing

that I can do

all by myself."

"What is that?" asked Frog.

"I can go home," said Toad.

"Winter may be beautiful,

but bed is much better."

The Corner

Frog and Toad

were caught in the rain.

They ran to Frog's house.

"I am all wet," said Toad.

"The day is spoiled."

"Have some tea and cake,"

said Frog. "The rain will stop.

If you stand near the stove,

your clothes will soon be dry.

18

I will tell you a story

while we are waiting," said Frog.

"Oh good," said Toad.

"When I was small,

not much bigger

than a pollywog," said Frog,

"my father said to me,

'Son, this is a cold, gray day

but spring

is just around the corner.'

20

I wanted spring to come.

I went out

to find that corner.

I walked down a path in the woods

until I came to a corner.

I went around the corner

to see if spring

was on the other side."

"And was it?" asked Toad.

"No," said Frog.

"There was only a pine tree,

three pebbles

and some dry grass.

I walked

in the meadow.

Soon I came to

another corner.

I went around the corner

to see if spring was there."

"Did you find it?" asked Toad.

"No," said Frog.

"There was only

an old worm

asleep on a

tree stump."

"I walked along the river

until I came to

another corner.

I went around the corner

to look for spring."

"Was it there?" asked Toad.

24

"No," said Frog.
"There was only
some wet mud
and a lizard who was chasing
his tail."
"You must have been tired,"
said Toad.
"I was tired," said Frog,
"and it started
to rain."

"I went back home.

When I got there," said Frog,

"I found another corner.

It was the corner of my house."

"Did you go around it?"

asked Toad.

"I went around that corner, too,"

said Frog.

"What did you see?"

asked Toad.

"I saw the sun coming out,"
said Frog. "I saw birds
sitting and singing in a tree.
I saw my mother and father
working in their garden.
I saw flowers in the garden."

27

"You found it!" cried Toad.

"Yes," said Frog.

"I was very happy.

I had found the corner

that spring was just around."

"Look, Frog," said Toad.

"You were right.

The rain has stopped."

Frog and Toad hurried outside.

28

They ran around the corner

of Frog's house

to make sure

that spring had come again.

Ice Cream

One hot summer day

Frog and Toad sat by the pond.

"I wish we had some

sweet, cold ice cream," said Frog.

"What a good idea," said Toad.

"Wait right here, Frog.

I will be back soon."

Toad went to the store.

He bought two big ice-cream cones.

Toad licked one of the cones.

"Frog likes chocolate best,"

said Toad, "and so do I."

Toad walked along the path.

A large, soft drop

of chocolate ice cream

slipped down his arm.

"This ice cream

is melting in the sun,"

said Toad.

Toad walked faster.

Many drops

of melting ice cream

flew through the air.

They fell down on Toad's head.

"I must hurry back

to Frog!" he cried.

More and more
of the ice cream
was melting.
It dripped down
on Toad's jacket.
It splattered
on his pants
and on his feet.
"Where is the path?"
cried Toad.
"I cannot see!"

Frog sat by the pond

waiting for Toad.

A mouse ran by.

"I just saw something awful!"

cried the mouse.

"It was big and brown!"

"Something covered
with sticks and leaves is moving
this way!" cried a squirrel.

"Here comes a thing with horns!"

shouted a rabbit.

"Run for your life!"

"What can it be?" asked Frog.

Frog hid behind a rock.

He saw the thing coming.

It was big and brown.

It was covered

with sticks and leaves.

It had two horns.

38

"Frog," cried the thing.

"Where are you?"

"Good heavens!"

said Frog.

"That thing is Toad!"

Toad fell into the pond.

He sank to the bottom

and came up again.

"Drat," said Toad.

"All of our sweet, cold ice cream

has washed away."

"Never mind," said Frog.

"I know what we can do."

Frog and Toad quickly ran back

to the store.

Then they sat in the shade

of a large tree

and ate

their chocolate

ice-cream cones

together.

The Surprise

It was October.

The leaves had fallen off

the trees.

They were lying on the ground.

"I will go to Toad's house,"

said Frog.

"I will rake all of the leaves

that have fallen on his lawn.

Toad will be surprised."

Frog took a rake

out of the

garden shed.

43

Toad looked out of his window.

"These messy leaves

have covered everything," said Toad.

He took a rake out of the closet.

"I will run over to Frog's house.

I will rake all of his leaves.

Frog will be very pleased."

Frog ran through the woods

so that Toad would not see him.

Toad ran through the high grass

so that Frog would not see him.

Frog came to Toad's house.

He looked in the window.

"Good," said Frog.

"Toad is out.

He will never know

who raked his leaves."

Toad got to Frog's house.

He looked in the window.

"Good," said Toad.

"Frog is not home.

He will never guess

who raked his leaves."

Frog worked hard.

He raked the leaves into a pile.

Soon Toad's lawn was clean.

Frog picked up his rake

and started home.

Toad pushed and pulled on the rake.

He raked the leaves into a pile.

Soon there was not a single leaf

in Frog's front yard.

Toad took his rake

and started home.

A wind came.

It blew across the land.

The pile of leaves

that Frog had raked for Toad

blew everywhere.

The pile of leaves

that Toad had raked for Frog

blew everywhere.

When Frog got home,

he said, "Tomorrow I will

clean up the leaves

that are all over my own lawn.

How surprised Toad must be!"

When Toad got home,

he said, "Tomorrow I will

get to work and rake

all of my own leaves.

How surprised Frog must be!"

That night
Frog and Toad
were both happy
when they each
turned out the light
and went to bed.

Christmas Eve

On Christmas Eve

Toad cooked a big dinner.

He decorated the tree.

"Frog is late," said Toad.

Toad looked at his clock.

He remembered it was broken.

The hands of the clock did not move.

Toad opened the front door.

He looked out into the night.

54

Frog was not there.

"I am worried,"

said Toad.

"What if something terrible
has happened?" said Toad.
"What if Frog has fallen
into a deep hole
and cannot get out?
I will never see him again!"

Toad opened the door once more.

Frog was not on the path.

"What if Frog is lost

in the woods?"

said Toad.

"What if

he is cold

and wet

and hungry?"

"What if Frog is being chased

by a big animal

with many sharp teeth?

What if he is being eaten up?"

cried Toad.

"My friend and I

will never have

another Christmas together!"

58

Toad found some rope in the cellar.

"I will pull Frog out of the hole

with this," said Toad.

Toad found a lantern in the attic.

"Frog will see this light.

I will show him the way

out of the woods," said Toad.

Toad found a frying pan

in the kitchen.

"I will hit that big animal

with this," said Toad.

"All of his teeth

will fall out.

Frog, do not worry," cried Toad.

"I am coming to help you!"

Toad ran out

of his house.

There was Frog.

"Hello, Toad," he said.

"I am very sorry to be late.

I was wrapping your present."

"You are not at the bottom

of a hole?" asked Toad.

"No," said Frog.

"You are not lost

in the woods?" asked Toad.

"No," said Frog.

"You are not being eaten

by a big animal?"

asked Toad.

"No," said Frog. "Not at all."

"Oh, Frog," said Toad,

"I am so glad to be

spending Christmas with you "

Toad opened his present from Frog.

It was a beautiful new clock.

The two friends sat by the fire.

The hands of the clock

moved to show the hours

of a merry Christmas Eve.